CALUMET CITY PUBLIC LIBRARY

3 1613 00378 3662

W9-AAV-494

BHT 17.00 4/68

# Fly, Monarch! Fly!

Written and Illustrated by

## Nancy Elizabeth Wallace

Marshall Cavendish Children

CALUMET CITY PUBLIC LIBRARY

Text and illustrations copyright © 2008 by Nancy Elizabeth Wallace

All rights reserved

Marshall Cavendish Corporation
99 White Plains Road
Tarrytown, NY 10591
www.marshallcavendish.us/kids

Library of Congress Cataloging-in-Publication Data
Wallace, Nancy Elizabeth.
Fly, monarch! Fly! / written and illustrated by
Nancy Elizabeth Wallace. — 1st ed.
p. cm.
ISBN 978-0-7614-5425-0
1. Monarch butterfly—Juvenile literature.  I. Title.
QL561.D3W35 2008
595.78'9—dc22
2007026624

The text of this book is set in Berling.
The artwork was created using origami and
found paper, markers, and acrylic paint.
Book design by Virginia Pope
Editor: Margery Cuyler
Art Director: Anahid Hamparian

Printed in Malaysia
First edition
1 3 5 6 4 2

mc Marshall Cavendish
Children

*Always, for Peter and my mom, Alexine,*

*and for children and adults everywhere—*
*may they be filled with the wonder and beauty of butterflies!*

*Special thanks to*
Carol Lemmon, co-founder and former president of the Connecticut Butterfly Association,
the staff of the entomology department at the Connecticut Agricultural Extension Service
*and* to Barbara Cangiano, Debby Trofatter and Jason Neely,
reference librarians at the James Blackstone Memorial Library in Branford, Connecticut

# Recipe
## ♥ Butterfly Sandwiches ♥

Ask an adult to help.

Make a sandwich with a filling you like.

Ask the adult to cut your sandwich in halves, then quarters, then eighths.

On a plate, arrange two of the sandwich triangles like wings. Add a carrot stick to the center for the body, half a cherry tomato or grape tomato for the head, and two thin celery sticks for the antennae.

One blue-sky day in late summer, Mom and Dad asked, "Who wants to go to Butterfly Place to visit the monarchs?"

"Me, me!" said Minna.

"Me!" shouted Pip.

They rode their bikes to Butterfly Place. The summer air smelled flower-sweet. The late summer sun warmed them.

Butterfly
Place
Where Monarchs Reign
→

They were greeted by the Butterfly Man. "Hello! I'm Bert. Welcome to Butterfly Place and the Milkweed Meadow."

"Hi, Bert!" said Minna and Pip.

"It's a great day for an egg hunt!" said Bert.

"An egg hunt?" asked Minna.

**Milkweed Meadow**

Welcome, Monarch Butterflies!

Save the milkweed =
Save the monarchs!!!

"Yes. Let's go look for butterfly eggs," said Bert. He handed them magnifying glasses. "You'll need these, because a female monarch's egg isn't much bigger than the head of a pin."

Minna started singing, "A-hunting we will go, a-hunting we will go . . ."

Female monarch laying one egg

Bert's Big Blue Bag

"Look, Minna! I'm an E–G–G!" shouted Pip.

EGG
STAGE

LASTS **4** TO **7** DAYS (depends on the weather)

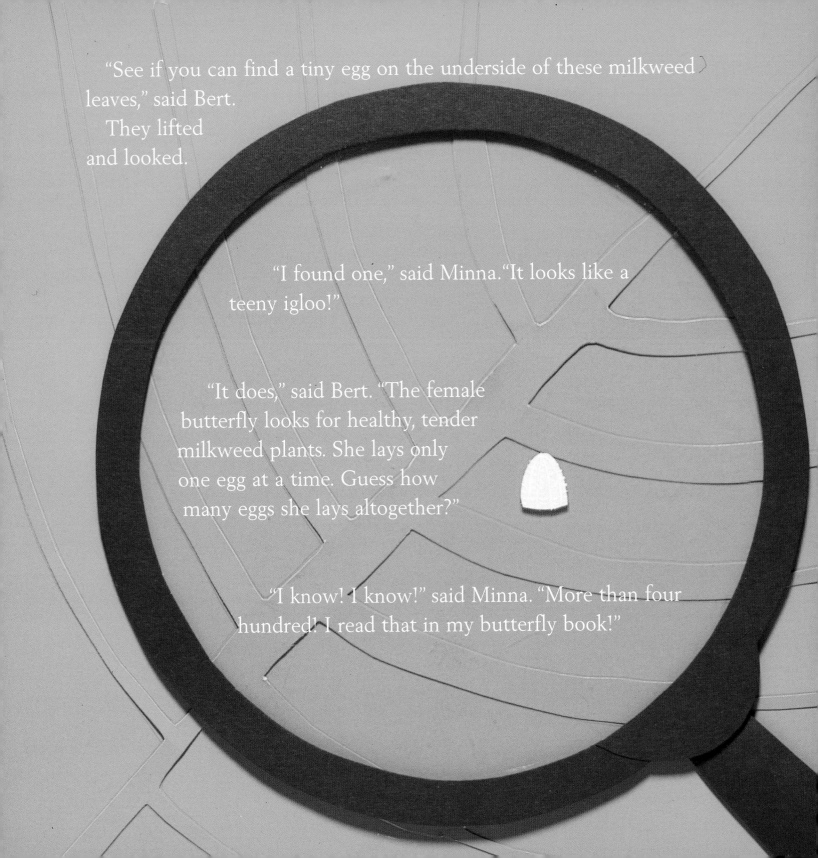

"See if you can find a tiny egg on the underside of these milkweed leaves," said Bert.
    They lifted and looked.

"I found one," said Minna. "It looks like a teeny igloo!"

"It does," said Bert. "The female butterfly looks for healthy, tender milkweed plants. She lays only one egg at a time. Guess how many eggs she lays altogether?"

"I know! I know!" said Minna. "More than four hundred! I read that in my butterfly book!"

Bert took a picture out of his big blue bag.

"When an egg is ready to hatch, a teeny tiny caterpillar nibbles a hole in the eggshell and wiggles out. The eggshell is the teeny tiny caterpillar's first meal."

"Ewww," said Minna.

"Sounds crunchy," said Dad.

Hatching caterpillar

Bert took a ruler with pictures on it out of his big blue bag.
  "The teeny tiny caterpillar munches milkweed, day and night, with its very strong jaws," said Bert. "It grows bigger . . ."

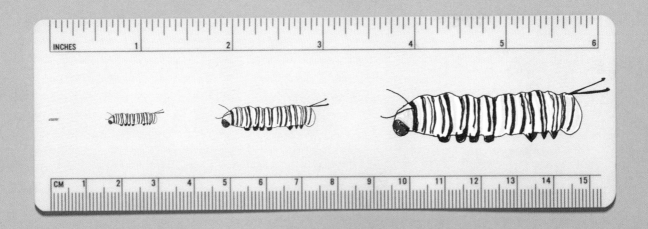

"and bigger and BIGGER!" Minna and Pip joined in.

Minna read:

Milkweed leaves provide food and protection. Milkweed has poisons in it, but they don't hurt the caterpillar. If another animal or bird tries to eat the caterpillar, the poisons make it taste terrible! The caterpillar's yellow, white, and black pattern tells predators to stay away.

"Look!" said Pip. "Now I'm a caterpillar!"
"And I'm a bird who wants to eat you up," said Dad.
"Stay away, bird! Stay away!" Pip giggled.

LARVA
(LAR-vuh)
STAGE

"THE CATERPILLAR STAGE"

LASTS 4 TO 7 DAYS (depends on the weather)

**Joke:** What did one monarch caterpillar say to another monarch caterpillar?

**Answer:** I want some *chocolate milk* weed!

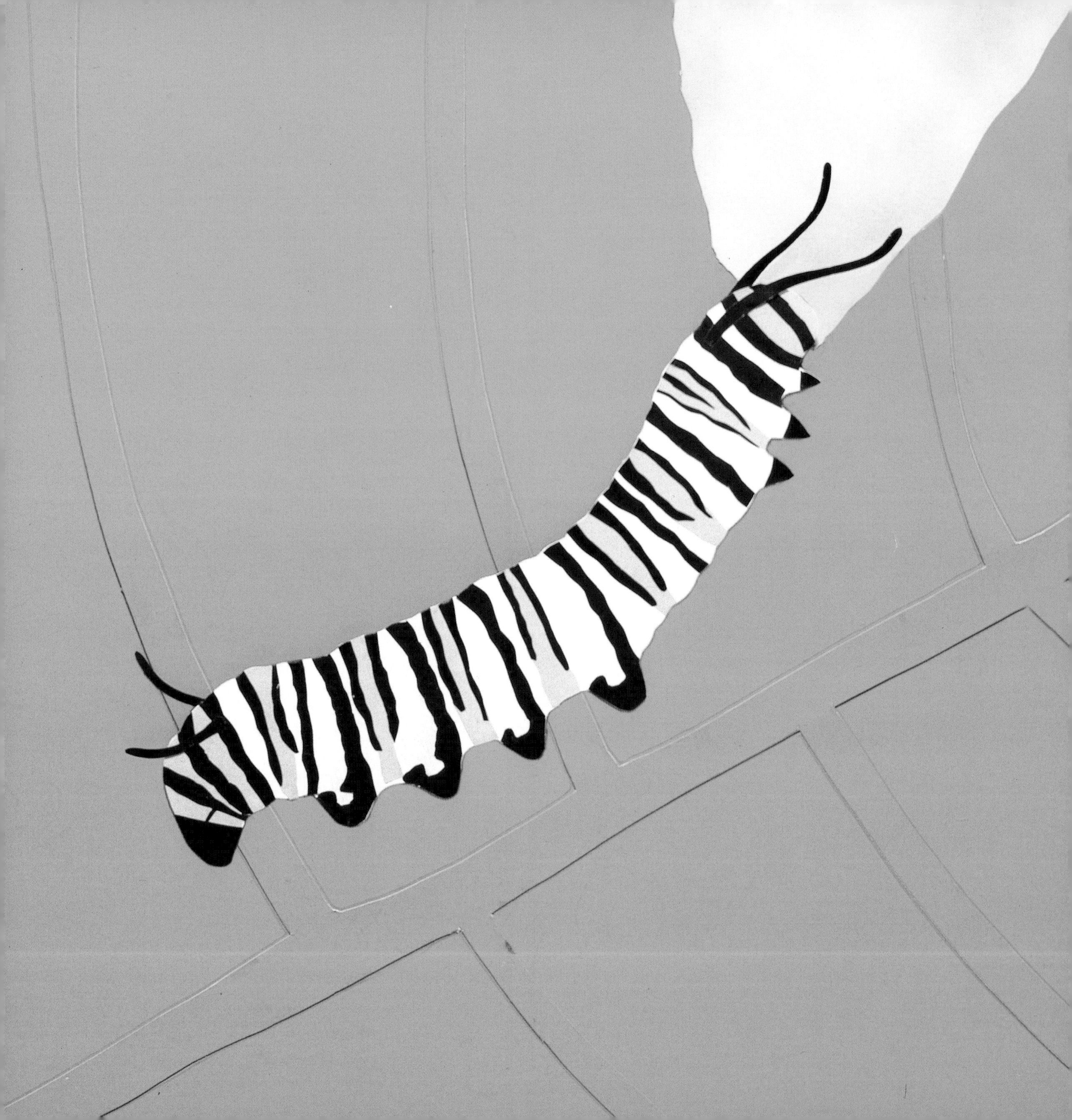

"I found a caterpillar!" said Minna. "It's yellow and black and white."

"Do you see the long black antennae, or feelers, on the head and the short antennae on the rear?" asked Bert.
"Yes," said Minna.

"Near the head, do you see three pairs of small true legs to walk with?"
"One. Two. Three," Minna counted. "I see more legs in back. They're stubby."

"Those are claspers," said Bert. "The caterpillar uses them to grip leaves."
"Cool!" said Minna.

Bert looked in his big blue bag. "Who wants to molt?"
"Me, me!" shouted Minna.

"Here, try this costume on," said Bert.

"Now *you're* a caterpillar, Minna!" said Pip.

"A caterpillar eats and grows," said Bert. "But its skin doesn't.

When the caterpillar grows too big for its outer skin, the tight skin splits open. The caterpillar wiggles and wriggles out. Underneath, there's new, larger skin. Shedding skin is called *molting*. The caterpillar usually molts four times."

"Then what happens, Bert?" asked Minna.

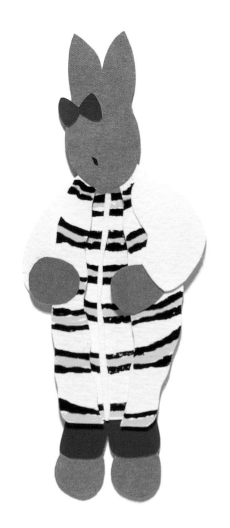

Bert reached into his big blue bag. He pulled out a stuffed-animal caterpillar.

"The fully grown caterpillar finds a safe place under a twig or leaf. Then it spins a silk pad using a special gland in its mouth called the *spinneret*. The caterpillar digs the tiny hooks on its rear end into the pad and swings head down. See if you can get the hooks into the white pad on this twig."

"We did it!" yelled Minna and Pip.

Bert took another picture out of his big blue bag. "The caterpillar sheds its skin for the last time."

"What happens next, Bert?" asked Dad.

"Follow me," said Bert.

caterpillar shedding skin

"It's not a caterpillar anymore," said Bert. "It's a *chrysalis*, or *pupa*."

"I see a PIP-A!"
said Minna. "And . . .
a tent. Let's go look!"

# PUPA
## STAGE

**CHRYSALIS** (KRIS-uh-lis) is another word for
**PUPA** (PEW-puh)

LASTS 5 TO 10 DAYS

Underneath the tent was a long table. On the table were three glass aquariums with net tops. Minna peered inside the first aquarium.

**PUPA** TENT
shelters the pupas
from the sun's heat

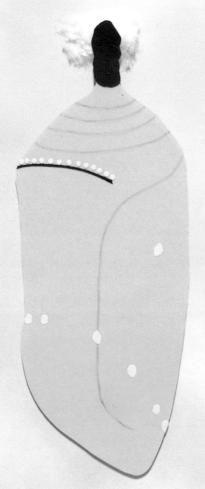

"I see something that looks like a beautiful green jewel!" said Minna.
Bert said, "That's a pupa. Amazing changes are happening inside."

Minna looked in the second aquarium.
"Wow! Wings!"

When she looked in the third aquarium, Minna shouted, "A butterfly!"

Bert said, "The butterfly works very hard to wriggle out. Then it pumps blood into its damp, crumpled wings until they unfold."

"What happens next, Bert?" asked Pip.

"The butterfly rests in the sun for a few hours so its wings will dry and harden. It's very important not to touch the butterfly until the wings have completely hardened," said Bert. "Let's go out to the butterfly garden. Oh, I forgot to tell you, be on the lookout for Big Sweetie."

"Big Sweetie?" shouted Minna and Pip.

3 1613 00378 3662

CALUMET CITY PUBLIC LIBRARY

"Is this Big Sweetie?" asked Minna.
"No," said Bert. "But you're
getting closer."

## ADULT
### STAGE
**"THE BUTTERFLY"**

LASTS 7 TO 10 DAYS
OR LASTS 7 TO 10 MONTHS
(if the adult migrates)

**Butterfly, butterfly,
flutter by, butterfly.
Flit, fly, and flutter by,
fleet-flying butterfly.**
*Say it fast three times.*

The poisons from eating milkweed in the LARVA/caterpillar stage are still in the ADULT/butterfly's body. The milkweed poisons now help protect the butterfly. If a bird takes a bite of a butterfly's wing, the poisons will make the bird sick!

The AMAZING change from

**EGG**

to

**LARVA**
(LAR-vuh)

to

**PUPA**
(PEW-puh)

to

**ADULT**

is called
**METAMORPHOSIS**
(me-tuh-MORE-fuh-sis)

Mom and Dad called, "Minna, Pip, come over here."

Minna stood very still. She whispered, "The butterfly is drinking nectar."

"What's nectar, Minna?" whispered Pip.

"Sweet flower juice! I read that in my butterfly book."

"Can you see the *proboscis*?" asked Bert. "It's like a built-in drinking straw. A butterfly drinks nectar with its proboscis."

They watched.

"The proboscis curls up when the butterfly isn't drinking. Here," said Bert. "A pretend proboscis for Minna, and one for Pip."

"Can I keep the party blower—I mean the pro-BAH-sis, Bert?" asked Minna. "You sure can," said Bert. "Let's keep strolling."

"Big Sweetie!"

**Big Sweetie**
sculpture
by Pierre Papillon

Dad read another sign:

A butterfly's compound eyes are made up of lots of little eyes. Butterflies can see more colors than any other creature on Earth. A butterfly smells with its feelers and tastes with its feet.

**Bert's Big Blue Bag**

Minna and Pip put on wings.

"When the colder fall weather arrives," said Bert, "millions of monarch butterflies fly south to Mexico and Southern California. They spend the winter where it's warmer. This journey is called *migration*. Monarchs migrate thousands of miles."

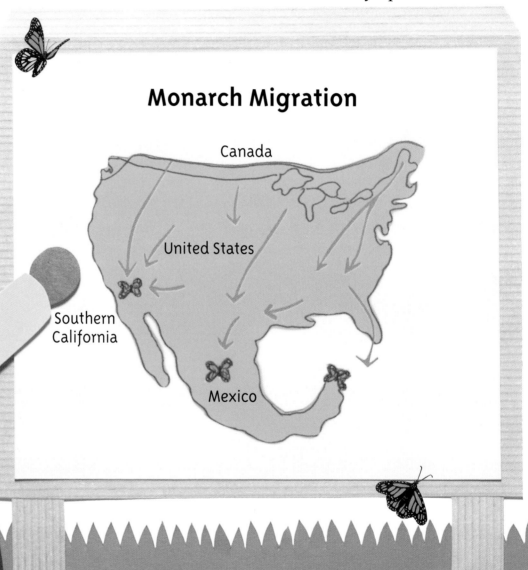

**Monarch Migration**

Canada

United States

Southern California

Mexico

"That's a long way to go for a butterfly," said Minna. "How do monarchs know how to get there, Bert?"

"They use the wind to help them. Their antennae help them know how strong the wind is blowing and what direction it's coming from. Monarchs migrate farther than any other kind of butterfly."

North

NW
NE

West
East

SW
SE

South

When the monarchs arrive in Mexico or Southern California, they cluster in trees in cool, moist places. They are much less active during the winter months. In the spring, males and females fly north again. On their journey, they drink nectar and water, they mate, and the females lay eggs. They stop to rest along the way.

Minna and Pip gave back the wings.
"Oh, one more thing," said Bert. "What if my last name was . . . Erfly."
Minna thought for a minute. "Your name would be . . . Bert Erfly!"
They all laughed.

"We had a great time! Thanks, Bert."

Bert said,
"Hope to see you
again soon."

**Bert's
Big Blue
Bag**

Joke: Why did the butter jump off the table?

Answer: It wanted to be a butterfly!

Butterfly Rock

The Puddle

# Minna's Monarch Magnet

**You will need:**

- orange card stock
- white paper
- a pencil
- a wide black marking pen

- safety scissors
- a hole puncher
- a glue stick
- a small piece of magnet tape

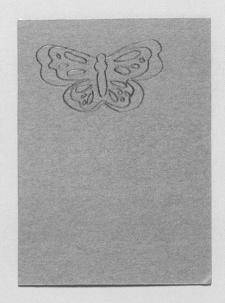

**1.** On the orange card stock, draw a butterfly and a pattern on the wings with the pencil.

**2.** Use the black marking pen to color the body and wing edges and to outline the pattern. Draw and color in a black rectangle on the card stock.

**3.** Cut out your butterfly with the scissors.

**4.** Cut out a pair of antennae from the black rectangle.

**5.** Punch circles in the white paper with the hole puncher.

**6.** Glue the circles onto your butterfly and glue the antennae onto your butterfly's head.

**7.** Attach a piece of magnet tape to the back of your butterfly. Stick your Monarch Magnet on the refrigerator.

# More about Monarchs

Monarchs are in the butterfly family called *milkweed butterflies*. Their genus and species names are *Danaus plexippus*!

Monarch butterflies are insects. All insects have bodies that are divided into three parts: head, thorax, and abdomen. All insects have three pairs of legs. Some insects, such as butterflies, bees, and flies, have wings.

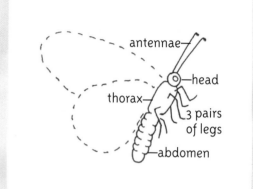

antennae

head

thorax

3 pairs of legs

abdomen

*Male Monarch*

*spots*

Male and female monarch butterflies look alike, except that male monarchs have two black spots on their wings.

*Viceroy butterflies* look a lot like monarch butterflies. When one animal looks like another animal or thing, it is said to "mimic" it. Viceroys don't taste bad, but enemies stay away because viceroys look like monarchs. They have a black line on each of their back wings.

*Viceroy*

No one knows for sure, but the orange, black, and white monarch butterfly may have been named *monarch* after a king of England—William of Orange. "Monarch" is another word for a king, queen, or emperor.

Monarchs are also called *tiger butterflies*.

# Plant Your Own Butterfly Garden

You can help monarchs! You can plant the milkweed that monarchs need for laying their eggs and that larvae/caterpillars need for food. You can plant all kinds of flowers that the adults/butterflies need for nectar.

Zinnia

Black-eyed Susan

Phlox

Aster

Butterflies need rocks for sunning themselves. The sun warms their muscles so they can fly.

Butterflies need water. Fill a shallow pan with a little water. Put a smooth, flat stone in it and set it in your garden.

# Where to Learn More about Monarchs!

Visit a butterfly conservatory!
There are butterfly conservatories in many states and Canadian provinces.

Visit a natural history museum!

Read other books about monarch butterflies!

Help tag monarchs at a
monarch-tagging
program!

Visit a botanical
garden!

Go to a monarch butterfly festival!